Bushbaby

Koala

Puppy

Kitten

Deer

Bear cub

Calf

Foal

Piglet

Lion cub

Dolphin

Duckling

Elephant

Fox cub

Kid

Hedgehog

Gibbon

Bat

Armadillo

Hippo

Joey

Mouse

owlet

Panda

Penguin chick

Meerkat

Rhino

Seal Pup

Lamb

cygnet

Turtle

Wolf Pup

Zebra

Chimpanzee

Lemur

Cassowary

Baboon

Gerbil

orang-utan

Gorilla

Blue Whale

Polar Bear cub

orca

otter

Leopard cub

Cheetah cub

Fennec fox

Tiger cub

Snow Leopard cub

Sea Lion Pup

Manatee

Giraffe

American Bison

Wildebeest

Howler Monkey

Possum

Dik Dik

Flamingo

Bald Eagle

Donkey

Toucan

Tortoise

Chameleon

crocodile

Rabbit

Whale Shark

Squirrel

Badger

Elephant Shrew

Weasel

Pelican

Tapir

Ostrich

Heron

Lynx cub

Spider Monkey

Wombat Baby

Thomson's Gazelle

Beaver

Skunk

Llama

Dromedary camel

Warthog

Aardvark

Puma cub

Marmoset

Hyena Cub

Mara

Raccoon

Sloth

Mongoose

Shark

Loris

Mandrill

Platypus

Guinea Pig

Chinchilla

Porcupine

Moose

Woodchuck

Arctic Hare